The Tailors a.k.a. The Stitchmans

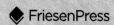 FriesenPress

One Printers Way
Altona, MB R0G 0B0
Canada

www.friesenpress.com

ISBN
978-1-03-914468-2 (Hardcover)
978-1-03-914467-5 (Paperback)
978-1-03-914469-9 (eBook)

1. Juvenile Fiction, Action & Adventure

Distributed to the trade by The Ingram Book Company

Thunder

and the Grizzly Bear Cub

Illustrated by Norm Clement

Written by
Rosie R. Stitchman
Samuel J. Stitchman
and James O. Stitchman

Dedications

To my mom, Thea Baturin; my dad, Brendan Stitchman; and my brother and best friend, Sam Stitchman.
Rosie R. Stitchman

To my mom, Thea Baturin; my dad, Brendan Stitchman; and my sister and best friend, Rosie Stitchman.
Samuel J. Stitchman

To my wife, Kathryn; my sons, David and Brendan; my grandchildren, Rosie and Sam; and my daughter-in-law, Thea Baturin, all of whom give me their unconditional love. You bring me endless happiness and make me so proud.
James O. Stitchman

Table of Contents

List of Characters

The Tailor Family

Rosie	Sam
Nana K	Papa J
Mom	Dad

Dude ranch personnel and law enforcement

Florence Marpole

Malcolm Marpole

Chief Growling Bear

Noah Spotted Wolf

Sheriff Pudding

Horses

Carrie	Larry
Mary	Thunder, a.k.a. Pipsqueak

Animals

Winnie, the rescue dog

Calypso, the grizzly bear cub

Dolores, the guard donkey

Outlaws

Lily Fisk

Louie Birch

Chapter 1
Winnie the Rescue Dog

It had been almost a year since Rosie, Sam, Nana K, and Papa J had returned from their amazing holiday at the Marpole Dude Ranch, in British Columbia. As promised, Papa J had replaced the silver crosses and chains that had been used by Chief Growling Bear for the bullets and spear tip on their last adventure. He also included a Star of David on each chain for additional good luck. As if on a secret signal, Rosie and Sam were often seen looking at each other and smiling; as they clutched their charms in their left hands and squeezed tightly. Papa J had also given Rosie and Sam a small pocket knife, like the one Sam had used to take the blackberry thorn from the mouth of the black horse, Thunder. Rosie's knife was red; Sam's was blue.

Over the summer, there was a new addition to the Tailor household. Rosie and Sam's Mom and Dad adopted a rescue dog from Mexico. The children had been asking, almost begging, to have a dog for several years. At last, their dream had come true, and that dream was a small dog named "Winnie".

In the fall when school started, their principal, having
heard of their heroic roles in what had become known as
the "Thunder and the Werewolves" adventure, asked them to
share their exploits with the entire school in the auditorium.

Nervously, they related the details of their exciting holiday and unexpectedly, they had become storytellers.

On a Saturday morning, the following May, even before the Tailors' doorbell rang; Rosie and Sam were standing at the door. Their canine alarm system had already signaled that someone was coming down the front walkway. Winnie had recognized Nana K and Papa J through the windows, and she was wiggling, while wagging her tail in anticipation of treats Papa J always had in his pockets for her.

When Nana K and Papa J had gotten comfortable in the living room, Nana K explained to the family that she had heard from Florence and Malcolm Marpole, owners of the dude ranch. Rosie, Sam, Nana K, and Papa J had been invited back to the ranch for the month of July. This would be a reward for Rosie and Sam's help in getting rid of the two werewolves last summer. It would also help get the ranch ready for the guests they would receive, once they reopened for the new season. There was a lot of work to be done; they needed experienced riders to exercise and groom their horses for the coming season. Rosie and Sam could easily help with those tasks. Nana K added that Florence had hinted a surprise was in store for them.

Rosie and Sam could hardly contain their excitement and began jumping around, hoping that Mom and Dad would allow them to accept this very generous gift. They were joined in their happy dance by Winnie, who had not even been invited.

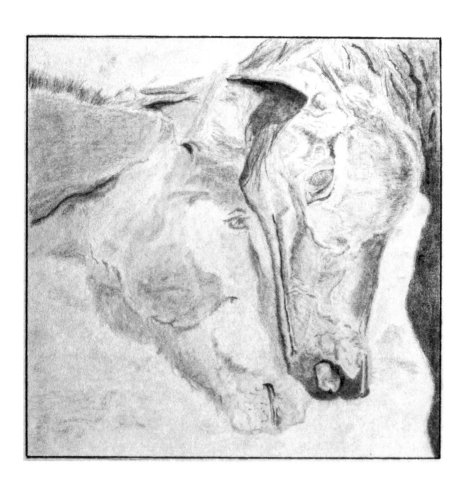

Chapter 2
The Trap Is Set

Once it was decided they would be returning to the ranch to work with Chief Growling Bear, plans would have to be made. Rosie and Sam could hardly wait to be caring again for their best friends, Thunder and Mary, as well as the other horses in the stable.

Nana K set up a virtual meeting with Florence; her husband, Malcolm; and of course, Chief Growling Bear. They outlined what kind of help Rosie, Sam, Nana K, and Papa J could provide over the month that they planned to stay at the ranch.

It would be another six weeks before their next adventure would begin. In the meantime, Rosie and Sam would work hard and finish their school year. They would continue to take their Taekwondo training lessons, attend soccer and baseball practices, and complete their usual chores around the house. They would also spend a lot of time training and playing with Winnie, their much-loved pup. It would be Mom and Dad's responsibility to keep the little hound safe and out of trouble once Rosie and Sam left for the ranch.

The weeks flew by, and soon it was time for Mom and Dad to drive Nana K, Papa J, Rosie, and Sam to the train station. Some tears were shed when Rosie and Sam hugged and kissed Winnie goodbye. More tears appeared as the train pulled away from the station, leaving Mom and Dad waving and shouting for the dudes to work hard, be safe, and have a great time. In no time, the mood on the train changed from tears to laughter as Rosie and Sam were soon playing a game of charades with Papa J, while Nana K read a book.

As the Tailors rode the train, two outlaws; named Lily Fisk and Louie Birch; were in the Great Bear Rainforest of British Columbia. They had been planning for weeks to steal a young grizzly bear cub from its mother to sell to a travelling circus.

Lily and Louie had arrived in the rainforest earlier that morning, driving a small pickup truck with an enclosed cargo area. They had already discovered a bears' cave on an earlier visit, where a mother grizzly lived with her two cubs; one male and one female. During that same visit, Lily had also spotted a large beehive stuffed full of honey, high up in a tree, close to the bears' den.

This morning, on the way to the cave, Louie climbed the tree, cut down the beehive, and secured it in a large garbage bag he had pricked with pin holes so the bees could breathe. The bag was then put in the cargo area of their truck, and Lily drove to a clearing not far from where the bears were still sleeping.

Lily and Louie then took the beehive out of the cargo area. Very, very carefully, they carried the buzzing bag towards the bears' home. As they approached, the hive was shaken from the bag and placed off to one side of the cave entrance. Lily and Louie then ran for their lives.

Chapter 3
The Grizzly Bear Cub Is Taken

Later that morning, when the three bears came out of their cave, the mother bear's nose was drawn straight to the beehive. She began gobbling up the honey, bees, and hive. The mother bear was so busy eating, she was unaware of the two outlaws watching close by.

Immediately Lily, who was hiding behind a tree, fired a small tranquilizer dart from her rifle. It struck the young female cub in the rump and put her to sleep. The thieves quickly loaded the sleeping cub into a big duffle bag and carried her to the back of their truck.

Only when the truck started to move away from the clearing did the mother bear realize that one of her babies had been taken. The mother bear rapidly led her little male cub back into the shelter of their den.

With Lily at the steering wheel, Louie was left to read the map they had drawn of the area, directing his partner out of the rainforest and back to the road. They had decided to use only the smaller paved roads and stay away from the main highways as much as possible.

The two thieves made their way back to the more densely populated area but wanted to bypass the small town of Turtleville. Louie directed Lily to take a dirt road that left their narrow, paved route and led back into the woods.

Once safely out of sight, they stopped the truck. Louie opened the cargo area and released the sleeping bear cub from the duffle bag. Now it could breathe more easily.

They soon began driving again, and it wasn't long before Lily misjudged a turn and drove off the side of the road into a puddle of soft mud. The small truck was not powerful enough to pull through the mud. They were stuck. The only choice they had was to leave the truck with the sleeping bear cub inside and walk back to the nearest town. There, they would steal another vehicle and some rope or chain they could use to tow their vehicle free of the mud.

Chapter 4
Best Friends Together Again

The trip seemed shorter this time for the Tailors, as
they recognized a lot of the scenery and buildings passing
by the train. Rather than take the bus from Turtleville to
the ranch, Malcolm and Florence had taken their station
wagon to collect the Tailors from the train station. Florence
explained to the Tailor family that Chief Growling Bear was
even more excited than Rosie and Sam to be working and
spending a whole month together.

Malcolm told the youngsters that Chief Growling Bear
had another First Nations friend visiting with him named
Noah Spotted Wolf. The two had grown up together in
British Columbia's Great Bear Rainforest, and as young men,
even joined the Canadian military at the same time. Chief
Growling Bear had been a medic, while Noah Spotted Wolf
had been a hand-to-hand combat trainer. They were both
very large and powerful men. Noah Spotted Wolf would be
helping Chief Growling Bear with the blacksmith chores.

Malcolm explained that the two blacksmiths would
be teaching Rosie and Sam about identifying tracks of

wild animals living around the ranch. They would also be showing them types of trees, plants, flowers, and bushes that made up part of British Columbia's interior. Much to Rosie and Sam's delight, horse whispering lessons would also be taught.

On the way to the Marpoles' ranch, Florence suggested they stop at the police station to visit with Sheriff Pudding. He had become a big fan of Rosie and Sam on their last holiday.

Sheriff Pudding welcomed the Tailor family back to his town and told them he would be by the ranch to spend some time with them. He was really looking forward to their visit.

While they were saying hello to Sheriff Pudding, Rosie noticed wanted posters for two horse and cattle thieves on the office wall.

Their names were Lily Fisk and Louie Birch, and she thought they were scary looking outlaws.

After their visit, everyone got back in the station wagon, and Malcolm hurried them home to an anxiously waiting Chief Growling Bear.

When they pulled into the driveway and stopped in front of the bunkhouse; Rosie and Sam scrambled from the vehicle and raced to the horse stable. Rosie went to Mary, and Sam, of course, ran straight to Thunder. As Malcolm had told them last year, these two horses had, in fact, become their best friends on the ranch.

Chapter 5
Back in the Saddle

Once the youngsters had hugged and scratched the necks of their best buddies, they then took off at a run to the barn to find Chief Growling Bear.

They raced into the barn and slid to a stop. There, stood Chief Growling Bear, wearing a wide grin, and holding out his arms like he was expecting the world's biggest hug from his two favourite cowpokes.

As the kids rushed to Chief Growling Bear, he put his big arms around the children and gave them a powerful squeeze. Rosie and Sam squealed with delight and hugged him back.

It was at this time that Noah Spotted Wolf came into the barn from a side door and was introduced to Rosie and Sam. Noah Spotted Wolf explained to Rosie and Sam that he and Chief Growling Bear had been out riding Thunder and Mary earlier that morning. They wanted to get the two horses ready for Sam and Rosie's visit.

He then told them he had just finished saddling up Thunder, Mary, Larry, and Carrie as Chief Growling Bear had asked. They would be taking Rosie and Sam out into the forest for a short ride before lunch.

Nana K and Papa J had big smiles on their faces as they watched their grandchildren ride off toward the forested area at the end of the ranch. Old and new friends, riding together.

The four riders left the ranch at the exact cedar tree where some of the excitement had started on their last visit. Both Rosie and Sam held their breath as they entered the wooded area that was just outside the boundary of Florence and Malcolm's property.

They had not ridden very far when Chief Growling Bear spotted something through the trees. He led them to a narrow dirt road that was not often used. Stuck in the mud, at the side of this road, they found a small truck. Noah Spotted Wolf dismounted and approached the vehicle.

The keys were still in the ignition, and Noah Spotted Wolf was stunned to see what was inside the cargo area. He called for Chief Growling Bear and the youngsters to come quickly.

Chapter 6
A Surprising Discovery

Noah Spotted Wolf suspected the young grizzly bear, sleeping in the back of the truck, was probably only three to five months old and had somehow been taken from its mother. He also told them the bear most likely came from the Great Bear Rainforest and would have to be returned. He added that he would advise the Wildlife Protection Agency of what they had found, and that he and Chief Growling Bear would be pleased to take care of the grizzly bear cub until the Agency made arrangements to have it returned to its home, in the rainforest.

Chief Growling Bear asked Rosie and Sam to return to the ranch with all the horses. He also asked that they have Papa J, and Nana K come back with them in the ranch's jeep. They would need to bring rope, chains, and a couple of long wooden planks to help free the truck from the mud.

With Sam on Thunder and Rosie on Mary, they led the other two horses back to the ranch. The two youngsters excitedly told Nana K, Papa J, Malcolm, and Florence of what they had found in the forest and what Chief Growling Bear and Noah Spotted Wolf needed.

Papa J, Nana K, Rosie, and Sam headed to the barn to load the jeep with all the gear that had been requested.

While waiting for the team to return, Chief Growling Bear and Noah Spotted Wolf carefully opened the cargo area to examine the young grizzly bear and make sure it was not hurt, only sleeping. They removed the tranquilizer dart that was still sticking out of its rump.

Once the others returned with the equipment, it did not take long to free the truck from the mud. With Noah Spotted Wolf behind the steering wheel of the truck, Nana K and Papa J jumped into the cab. Chief Growling Bear drove the jeep, with Sam and Rosie on the seat beside him. Both Rosie and Sam's eyes were fixed on the back of the truck where the young grizzly bear was held, still asleep. Chief Growling Bear, Rosie, and Sam were finally a "team" again.

As they drove along, Rosie wondered to herself about the heavy work boot treads she had noticed at the edges of the mud puddle. She did not think they belonged to anyone in her group. Whose prints could they be? she wondered.

At this same moment, Nana K noticed a drawing taped to the dashboard of the truck. It looked very similar to a treasure map, just like the ones that Papa J used to draw up for Rosie and Sam when they were younger, for their homemade treasure hunts. It was a drawing with directions of exactly where in the rainforest the bears' den was located. It was the map that Lily and Louie had made to be able to return to the cave on the day of the theft. Nana K folded the map and handed it to Papa J to put in his shirt pocket for later use.

As the Tailors, Chief Growling Bear, and Noah Spotted Wolf drove away from the mud puddle site, Lily Fisk and Louie Birch were just returning with a van they had stolen. They had brought ropes and chains they thought they would need to get their small truck out of the mud. They approached from the opposite direction and saw the tail end of their small truck and the ranch's jeep disappear around a corner in the road on the way out of the forest. The outlaws couldn't believe it. Lily shouted, "They've stolen our bear!!!"

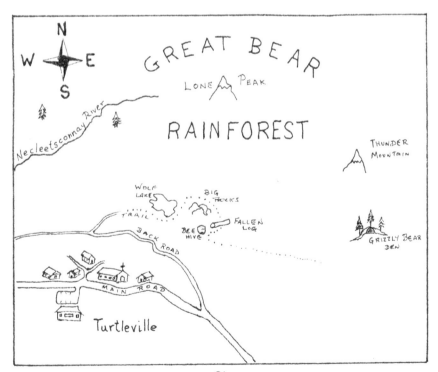

Chapter 7
The Training Begins

Lily and Louie kept their van far enough back to allow them to follow the two vehicles without being seen. As the small truck and jeep pulled into the driveway leading to the Marpoles' ranch, Lily and Louis continued driving straight past the entrance. This way, it would not appear that they had been following them.

The outlaws drove several miles further along the road, before they came to a parking area, where they could stop and discuss what had happened and what their next move would be. This adventure of theirs had just become a lot more complicated.

The first thing they thought to do was to go back towards the ranch and find a place to hide their vehicle. They would then sneak around the ranch and find out who was involved in the theft of their bear cub.

Over the next three days, Lily and Louie skulked behind bushes, hid behind rocks, and even climbed trees to get better views of what was going on at the ranch.

They discovered that the bear cub was being kept in a stall between two horses in the stable.

Each morning, Chief Growling Bear, Noah Spotted Wolf, Rosie, and Sam would go to the stable and bring the bear cub and their two horses into the big barn. Once there, the bear cub would be fed a breakfast of fish, plants, roots, fruits, and berries. Mary and Thunder would have a sizable bag of grass clippings and then share berries with the bear cub.

Lily and Louie decided that the best place to steal the bear cub back would be to take her right out of the barn; after she had eaten breakfast. They would use one of the two remaining tranquilizer darts and then place the cub in the extra duffle bag that they had brought with them.

The first thing that Noah Spotted Wolf had done upon his return from the forest was to call the Wildlife Protection Agency and report the bear cub in their possession and how they had found the cub in the woods. The authorities told him they would visit the ranch later that day. When two officers from the Wildlife Protection Agency showed up, they were impressed with what had already been done for the little bear cub. Seeing that it was in good health, they asked Malcolm, Chief Growling Bear, and Noah Spotted Wolf if they would provide care and safe-keeping for the bear cub for a few more days. Papa J gave the "treasure map" that Nana K had found to them. The officers said that they would investigate the location of the cave to be sure the mother bear was still there.

Rosie and Sam started each morning by dressing in their Taekwondo gis and practicing their moves, jumps, punches, and kicks on the grass outside the barn.

They began to help with the chores they had agreed to do for Florence, Malcolm, and Chief Growling Bear. It still left lots of time for them to groom and ride Thunder, Mary, as well as the other horses. It also allowed time for them to be taught about the trees, bushes, flowers, shrubs, and plants in the forest. It gave Noah Spotted Wolf and Chief Growling Bear time to teach Rosie and Sam about the many animals living in the forest and how to recognize the different tracks animals left on the ground or on the bark of trees. Noah Spotted Wolf also began the promised "horse whisperer" lessons.

As the lessons went on, it occurred to Rosie to tell the others about the boot tracks she had noticed at the mud puddle back in the forest. Chief Growling Bear told Rosie that those tracks probably belonged to the thieves who had abandoned the small truck.

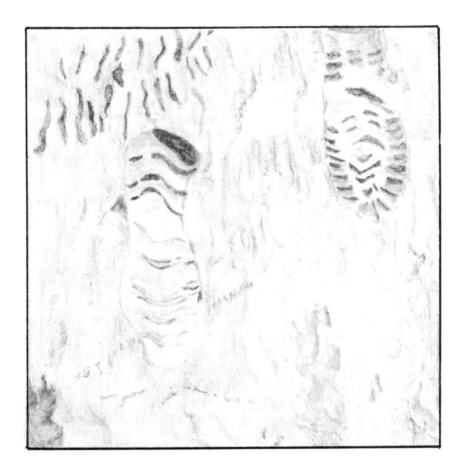

Chapter 8
Louie Birch Underestimates Sam

Each day, before and after riding, Rosie and Sam brought Mary and Thunder into the barn, under the guidance of Chief Growling Bear and Noah Spotted Wolf, to visit with the grizzly bear cub. The horses were quite nervous at first but, after each visit, they seemed to be less frightened and more curious. Chief Growling Bear and Noah Spotted Wolf used these occasions to teach Rosie and Sam more details of becoming "horse whisperers".

The bear cub was kept extremely well fed, and being so young, did not appear to be aggressive towards, or afraid of, the horses or the youngsters.

One morning Rosie asked Chief Growling Bear and Noah Spotted Wolf if she could pick out a name for the young bear. They laughed and told Rosie that it was an excellent idea. They also told her to remember that this bear would grow to be a very powerful critter and to please not pick a name like "Buttercup".

Rosie looked at Sam and smiled. They still had not changed from their gis after practicing Taekwondo. They both took their charms in their left hands and squeezed tightly as Rosie said that they had chosen "Calypso" as the name for this magnificent little grizzly bear.

Morning breakfasts together allowed Calypso, Mary, and Thunder to become a small family. Calypso and Thunder would rub noses to show the growing trust between one another. Mary appeared shyer and although no longer afraid of the little bear, did not seem to be as comfortable as the big black horse.

One morning, after breakfast in the barn, Chief Growling Bear asked Sam to please go to the ranch house and get Nana K and Papa J. He also asked Sam to bring the picnic lunches, which Florence and Malcolm had prepared for them, since they would be spending the rest of the morning out in the forest "tracking". "Take Thunder with you," suggested Chief Growling Bear.

Louie left Lily with the van, hidden in some bushes behind the barn. She was to stay out of sight until he called for her to help carry the duffle bag, once the bear had been tranquilized. Meanwhile, Louie was going to the ranch house to see if the coast was clear. As he snuck around on the porch looking in through the kitchen windows, he heard the young boy coming from the barn with a horse. Louie hid behind a big cedar chest which was kept on the porch to store firewood. As Sam jumped onto the porch to enter the kitchen, he noticed some muddy boot prints very much like the ones Rosie had described seeing in the forest at the mud puddle. Upon seeing the footprints, Sam followed them to the chest where Louie jumped out waving his tranquilizer rifle wildly over his head.

Sam took two quick steps toward Louie, leaped into the air, and gave Louie a solid Taekwondo front kick to the chest. Thanks to Sam's several years of training with Master Paul, his kick was powerful enough to knock Louie backward off the end of the porch into Florence's cactus garden and onto a rather large prickly pear cactus.

The howling was immediate, and the pain was unbearable. Louie was unable to get off the cactus. Every time he tried to place his hands for support or to push himself up, it ended with more and more needles being stuck in his hands, arms, legs and body. It did not help him that Thunder had raced around the porch and into the cactus patch. Each time Louie moved, Thunder placed his long face on Louie's chest and held him, stopping him from making any progress. Louie had to lay still, just suffer the pain and continue to scream for help. Nana K, Papa J, Florence, and Malcolm came rushing from the kitchen wondering what was going on.

Louie had lost his rifle with the dart loaded in it when he was kicked and fell into the garden. Sam picked up the rifle and carefully handed it to Malcolm.

Louie's screams were heard as far away as the barn. Chief Growling Bear asked Rosie to please go to the ranch house and make sure everyone was all right.

Chapter 9
Lily Fisk Is No Match for Rosie

As Rosie left the barn, Lily, hearing the same noises, left the van to go and see if Louie needed any help.

Lily spotted Rosie and grabbed her by the wrist. Rosie, taken by surprise, quickly pulled and rotated her hand and arm, breaking free from Lily's grip, just like Master Paul had taught her at Taekwondo class.

Rosie quickly recognized the woman as being the same one on the wanted poster in Sheriff Pudding's office. As Lily stepped forward, she reached for Rosie again. Without hesitation and with her left foot planted firmly on the ground, Rosie administered a thundering heel kick to the tip of Lily's chin. The kick was so forceful that it dazed and knocked Lily backward and down onto her butt. Once again, Master Paul would be pleased and proud of his young Taekwondo student.

More bad news for Lily was that she had put the last spare tranquilizer dart in her back pocket. She now landed on the dart with the tip sticking into her rump.

Rosie ran back to the barn and quickly told Chief Growling Bear and Noah Spotted Wolf what had just happened.

Noah Spotted Wolf immediately led Mary and Calypso back to their stalls in the stable for safety.

Chief Growling Bear took a length of rope from the workbench and raced to Lily Fisk to make sure she did not get away. There was no need to hurry, as by the time he got to her, she was sound asleep. Chief Growling Bear was not sure if it was from the medication in the dart or from the kick that Rosie had delivered. The rope was tied to Lily's wrists; she was then rolled onto her side for safekeeping to await the arrival of Sheriff Pudding.

After Noah Spotted Wolf had secured Mary and Calypso in their stalls, he hustled to the ranch house where Sam was standing on the porch watching over Thunder while Louie struggled with the prickly pear cactus plant.

Chief Growling Bear and Rosie made their way to the ranch house and asked Papa J to please call Sheriff Pudding, as they had captured two bear thieves who needed to book rooms in his jail.

Sam and Rosie then took Thunder, back to his stall in the stable, while the rest of the group extracted Louie from the cactus garden. Florence, Malcolm, and Nana K stood on the porch watching in disbelief. Louie was tied up by Noah Spotted Wolf and marched towards the barn. He was placed on the ground, outside the barn, beside his sleeping partner.

Rosie, Sam, Florence, Malcolm, Papa J, and Nana K joined them at the barn entrance. There was the sound of a vehicle approaching; everyone's gaze turned to the driveway. It was Sheriff Pudding, and his deputy arriving to arrest the two bear-nappers and take them to jail. Sheriff Pudding said hello to everyone and shook Rosie and Sam's hands once he heard the story of how the outlaws had been captured. He told Malcolm and Florence they were lucky to have such tough, loyal friends to help out on the ranch. It was the first time he had seen heroes, dressed in Taekwondo gis, on a dude ranch.

Chapter 10
Good to Be Going Home

Sheriff Pudding and his deputy left with their two prisoners, while Rosie and Sam returned to the bunkhouse to change into their ranch clothes. Shortly after, the sound of another vehicle coming up the driveway to the ranch got everyone's attention. It was the Wildlife Protection Agency officers coming to collect the little grizzly bear cub.

Malcolm directed the two officers to pull their van up beside the door to the stable. Chief Growling Bear and Noah Spotted Wolf went into the stable to get Calypso. They had made a leather collar and leash to allow them to direct the small bear out of the barn, leading her into the back of the van. A cage had been placed in the van to help protect the cub on the trip back home. The cage was now being stocked by Rosie and Sam with some of the bear cub's favourite berries. They thought it would make the trip home a little more bearable for their dear Calypso. As Calypso passed Thunder's stall, the big horse leaned down to rub noses with the grizzly bear cub one last time.

There were tears in everyone's eyes as Calypso was walked to the van. Rosie and Sam approached and gave the little cub a scratch behind each ear and a pat on her rump. The little cub licked each of the youngsters on the back of their hands as if to thank them for saving her.

With that, the Wildlife Protection Agency officers thanked everyone again for their help and care of the little bear. They said they would try to get a photo of the grizzly bear family once they were together again. The officers promised to send a copy of the picture to Rosie and Sam and then they were off. Calypso could be seen enjoying her snack through the windows of the van as it moved down the driveway.

Chief Growling Bear put his arms around Rosie and Sam and hugged them as the vehicle drove away. Noah Spotted Wolf reminded them that Calypso was on her way back to the rainforest and to her life as a true grizzly bear. Noah Spotted Wolf told Rosie and Sam that, because they had been so kind to, and protective of Calypso, part of the little bear's spirit would always remain in their hearts.

The tears dried, but everyone was still moving in slow motion. They were disappointed that Calypso was gone yet happy that she was heading home to be with her mom.

Suddenly, they heard the sound of yet another vehicle coming from the driveway where the Wildlife Protection Agency's van had just disappeared.

Chapter 11
Florence's Lambs Arrive

Rosie and Sam raced to the driveway to see what was going on. Chief Growling Bear smiled and shouted to them that it was probably the lambs and guard donkey Florence had arranged to have delivered for the summer activities.

Noah Spotted Wolf suggested they would now have to come up with another name for the new guard donkey. Rosie piped up immediately saying that "Dolores" would be a perfect name for the newest addition to the Marpole ranch's security team.

Rosie, Sam, and Noah Spotted Wolf watched as the driver stopped beside the barn and opened the back door of the truck. The driver then placed a ramp leading from the back of his truck to the ground. Immediately, little lambs began racing down the ramp and into the barnyard, disappearing around the back of the barn. The guard donkey was right behind them.

Noah Spotted Wolf let out a yell and raced behind the barn to try and contain the lambs, with Rosie and Sam right on his heels. Noah Spotted Wolf bent forward at the waist to make eye contact with the donkey. He began heading towards Dolores the guard donkey, shouting loudly at her. He had only taken a few steps when Dolores put her head down and charged at Noah Spotted Wolf. The donkey struck Noah Spotted Wolf in the chest with her forehead, knocking him backwards, head over heels. Noah Spotted Wolf quickly jumped up, ran to pick up his displaced eagle feather, and returned to the barnyard muttering and complaining about the stubborn, unruly donkey. He called to the youngsters to be careful and to give the guard donkey lots of room.

Rosie and Sam continued rounding up the little lambs and as Sam led them back around the barn to the barnyard, Rosie made a beeline for Dolores. Rosie walked slowly, with her left arm stretched out towards the donkey. She whispered Dolores's name and spoke very quietly. The donkey had to strain and pay attention to hear what Rosie was saying.

When Rosie got close enough to reach up and take hold of the donkey's bridle, she began scratching Dolores's ear. The donkey seemed to like the treatment that this little person was giving her. Rosie continued to speak softly into Dolores's ear. Suddenly, the donkey dropped to her two front knees and nuzzled Rosie with her nose.

Rosie, still holding the bridle with her left hand, grabbed the tuft of hair between Dolores's ears with her right hand and swung her right leg up and over the donkey's back. The donkey immediately stood and began slowly walking around to the front of the barn.

Just as Noah Spotted Wolf was explaining to the others, for the third time, how wild and untrained the new guard donkey was, Dolores and Rosie came into view.

The laughing was immediate and the applause began slowly and then got louder. Even Noah Spotted Wolf joined in the applause with a big smile when Chief Growling Bear shouted that Noah Spotted Wolf must be a better teacher of horse whispering than anyone imagined.

With Rosie on Dolores's back and Sam helping to round up the stragglers, the lambs were shepherded across the barnyard. They were placed in a small grassy field that had been prepared for them.

Chapter 12
Getting Ready for the Trip Home

The ranch was a less hectic place now that the little bear cub had been returned to the rainforest and the outlaws had been caught and safely locked up in jail. Rosie and Sam continued with the training that Chief Growling Bear and Noah Spotted Wolf had started. They also returned to doing their chores in caring for the horses, lambs, and guard donkey. There did not seem to be much time for resting and relaxing in the days ahead.

Rosie and Sam truly enjoyed taking care of the lambs. Rosie and Dolores already appeared to be good friends. Rosie made a habit of getting Mary from the stable and taking her into the field to graze on grass while they spent time with all her lambs and Dolores. They were all becoming the best of friends.

Sam spent as much time as he could with Thunder. They were often seen riding around the ranch after all the chores were done.

They stopped frequently and Sam could be seen using his new horse whispering skills with his trusting friend, while he patted and spoiled the big horse with sugar cubes, apples, and carrots.

Chief Growling Bear and Noah Spotted Wolf continued the lessons of identifying animal tracks, types of trees, flowers, and bushes. The youngsters were shown which types of berries, mushrooms, and shoots were safe to eat.

Noah Spotted Wolf brought some deerskin to the barn one afternoon. He was going to teach Rosie and Sam how to make moccasins, which would allow them to move around more quietly. This would allow them to get closer to the animals they wanted to watch and admire. Chief Growling Bear taught them how to approach animals from "downwind", so the breeze would not blow their scent to the animals they were tracking.

It did not take long for Rosie and Sam to master how to walk around as silently as ghosts. Their friends and teachers, Chief Growling Bear and Noah Spotted Wolf, were having trouble keeping track of where and when the youngsters entered the ranch house, barn, or stable. This, they said, was the true test of their hunting and tracking abilities.

Just before dinner one night at the ranch, an envelope arrived by express delivery. Inside was a photo of an enormous mother grizzly bear with not one, but two baby cubs. They were outside a small cave, and the mother grizzly was licking one of the cubs all over as it lay on its back. The other little cub was sitting as close as possible to the one being licked by its mother.

Rosie and Sam realized immediately that it was Calypso
with her mother, and that there was another brother or sister
in the family.

Once again, Rosie and Sam clutched their charms in their left hands and squeezed tightly, while smiling at each other.

The day came too quickly for them to pack their bags and head home. Hands were shaken, hugs were exchanged, and again a few tears were shed.

The Marpoles were very pleased with all the help the Tailors had provided over the past month. As a thank you, Florence surprised them by saying that she had been speaking to Nana K about the possibility of them returning again next summer. Nana K said that she had already spoken to Rosie and Sam's parents and it could very well happen. Papa J spoke up; he did not know if he could take another summer of excitement like what always seemed to happen at this ranch. Nana K simply said, "Papa J, get over it. The grandkids love being here". With that said, all Papa J could say was "Que sera, sera" (what will be, will be).

Chief Growling Bear and Noah Spotted Wolf smiled and nodded knowingly.

The Tailors were driven back to the train station by Malcolm and Florence. The train ride seemed shorter than the last time. They talked and shared their favourite parts of their working holiday.

Mom and Dad were at the train station in Vancouver waiting for them. The car ride home was loud and exciting. As they approached their house, Rosie asked, "May we please be dropped off at the corner of our street?"

Rosie and Sam were wearing their moccasins and wanted to try to surprise Winnie. By the time Mom and Dad came in through the front door with the luggage, Winnie was going wild. Unbeknownst to Winnie, Rosie and Sam were already sitting on the sofa in the living room. Their moccasins and ghostly talents seemed to work.

The End

Acknowledgements

We would like to thank Anne and Gord Riddick, Beth and Jim Amirault, Norm Clement, Jamie Ross, and Kathryn Stitchman for their encouragement, suggestions, and friendship.

Double tip of the hat to Anne Riddick, Beth Amirault, Claire Clement, Brendan Stitchman, and Kathryn Stitchman, for their tremendous editing powers and comprehension of the English language.

Last, but certainly not least, our undying appreciation to Norm Clement, for help with editing and providing the illustrations for our little story, and to Thea Baturin and Brendan Stitchman, for the photography included in this book.

Rosie and Nana K

Rosie R., James O. and Samuel J. Stitchman

About the Authors

James Stitchman, the inspiration behind Papa J Tailor, has spent his lifetime coaching, teaching, and interacting with children through various amateur sports involvement. A natural story-teller, he would share stories with the community children, as well as his grandchildren, Rosie and Sam. As Rosie and Sam grew, they began adding to their grandfather's stories, and the three let their imaginations run wild. From that, the "Rosie and Sam's Dude Ranch Adventures" series was born. A follow-up to Thunder and the Werewolves, published in 2021, the Stitchman grandfather and grandchildren writing team have reunited to pen Thunder and the Grizzly Bear Cub, the second book in the "Rosie and Sam's Dude Ranch Adventures" series.

Rosie and Samuel live in North Vancouver, British Columbia with their mom, Thea; their dad, Brendan; and their rescue dog, Winnie.

James lives in Vancouver, British Columbia with his wife Kathryn.